# The
# Very Sensitive Princess
## By Linda Slomin

Cover Design, Illustrations & Formatting
by George Perez

This book is inspired by the story of
*The Princess and the Pea,*
by Hans Christian Anderson,
and is in the public domain.

All scripture references taken from
Easy-to-Read Version Bible,
Copyright © 2006 by
Bible League International.

The author can be reached at
lmslomin@gmail.com
ISBN 979-8-6317-0251-6

# Acknowledgements & Dedication

I honestly don't remember who introduced me to the story of *The Princess and the Pea*, but it was one of my favorite fairy tales growing up. I would like to thank Pastor Paul Scull who has been a mentor to me as a Christian and now as an author. Secondly, Pastor Tony Cotto helped me to revise the first draft of this book into a more creative story. George Perez is a beloved family friend who is not only my illustrator, but was also in our wedding.

Next, Dr. Mary Ann Diorio is an author who read my manuscript and offered advice, and I will always remember her as an intercessor for me when I was on a missionary trip in India. Kathryn Ross is a publisher who graciously invited me to her writer's group where a group of authors red-inked my manuscript. Thank you for including me in your circle of loving friends.

And I thank God who gave me the idea to write this book after I used the story a few times in a puppet show while on a couple of missionary trips. I played Princess Pheona and Gabriel Carr played Reggie.

I dedicate this book to Kai Slomin, the recent addition to our family. At the writing of this book my grandson is three years old and he is the love of our lives, truly a blessing from the Lord!

# Puppets used on mission trips

Original
Princess Pheona puppet

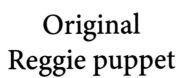

Original
Reggie puppet

Princess Pheona and Reggie were best friends.
They played outside every day on the soft, green grass.
It felt gentle on the Princess's very sensitive skin.
Reggie was the son of Mr. Peebles, one of the
King's servants, and they lived in the castle too.

"Bye, Reggie. I'm so tired from playing today that
I can't wait to eat dinner and fall asleep!
Tomorrow is going to be a very special day!"
"Bye, Princess Pheona. Tomorrow is the big celebration
in the kingdom. I'm really looking forward to it!"

5

After dinner with the King and the Queen,
Princess Pheona slipped into bed, sighed, and fell right to sleep.
But then ... "Ouch!" she said.
"I feel something lumpy and kind of bumpy
underneath my mattress."

"Mommy, wake up. I feel something lumpy and kinda bumpy underneath my mattress."
The Queen yawned. "Something lumpy and kinda bumpy? Hmm. What can we do?
I know! We can get Mr. Peebles to put a fluffy, puffy mattress on top of the first one."

The Queen and Princess Pheona woke up Mr. Peebles.
Reggie came too.
"Here's a fluffy, puffy mattress for you, Princess Pheona.
I hope you can sleep now without feeling something
lumpy and kinda bumpy underneath your mattress."

The Princess plopped herself on her fluffy, puffy mattress
and fell asleep. But then... "Ouch! I feel something lumpy
and kinda bumpy underneath my mattress!"
She twisted and turned and popped right out of bed.
The Princess ran off to the Queen's bedroom a second time.

Princess Pheona gently shook the Queen once again and moaned, "Mommy, I can't sleep. I feel something lumpy and kinda bumpy underneath my mattress."

The Queen thought harder this time.

"I have an idea. Mr. Peebles, please put a third mattress on Pheona's bed. Surely the Princess will feel better this time."

Mr. Peebles put another fluffy, puffy mattress on top of the other two.

"My bed is really getting high now!" shouted the Princess.

Once again, Princess Pheona fell right to sleep. But within minutes
she twisted and turned and popped right out of bed!
She ran into the Queen's room crying.
Her tears fell on her Mommy's face. The Queen was sad.
"Oh dear. I've got to think harder! I know!
I'll ask Mr. Peebles to give you a total of ten fluffy, puffy mattresses!"

11

"My bed is so high it almost touches the sky!
I even have to use a ladder to climb up there!"
Reggie said, "Surely this time you'll be able to fall right to sleep.
You won't feel anything lumpy and kinda bumpy
underneath your mattress."
"Now go to sleep, Princess Pheona. We all need to get some
rest for tomorrow!" said Mr. Peebles.

The Princess yawned with an extra loud yawn.
"Surely I will fall asleep and *stay* asleep this time!" But no!
The Princess twisted and turned and popped right out of bed!
"Oh, no! I feel something lumpy and kinda bumpy
underneath my mattress. What shall I do now?
I know! I will wake up Daddy. He'll know what to do."

13

"What's wrong my sweet, little Princess?" asked the King.
Princess Pheona explained the whole story to her father,
a King of great wisdom. The King put on his royal robe and walked
over to Princess Pheona's bedroom.
"Mr. Peebles, please take all of the fluffy, puffy mattresses off of
Princess Pheona's bed, even the very bottom one.
Let's see what is underneath the first mattress that is
making her feel so lumpy and kinda bumpy."

14

The King was the first one to see what the problem was
and he chuckled.
"Princess Pheona, guess what was
underneath your mattress?" giggled Reggie.
"A baby doll? A squirmy mouse? A high stack of money?
I don't know, Reggie! What is it??!!"
"A pea."
"A pea?"
"A pea. You felt that even when ten mattresses were on top of it?!"
"Yes. I am very sensitive."

"Hmm.
That reminds me of something, Princess Pheona."
"What Daddy?"
"Well, that's the way sin works."

Princess Pheona asked, "What do you mean by sin, Daddy?"
"It's the things that we do that make God sad."
"Oh, like the time Mommy asked me to clean my room and instead I hid everything under my bed."
"I sinned when I pulled my sister's hair and called her mean names," added Reggie.

"We all sin. Everyone in the whole world sins from little kids to adults," explained the King.

"So how does the Princess being sensitive to a pea remind you of sin?" wondered Reggie out loud.

The King explained, "When we sin we feel uncomfortable on the inside."

"Just like I felt uncomfortable on the mattress with the pea underneath it," said Princess Pheona.

18

"I don't like sin. I want to hide from God when I sin," said Reggie.
"Yes, it makes you feel afraid to talk to God, but God wants
to forgive you," said the King.
"So how do we get rid of it?" asked Reggie.

"There is only one way and only one person who can help us with that," said the wise King.
"Is it to get help from you, Daddy? You solved my problem with the pea."
"No dear. That kind of help doesn't come from me, a King who lives on earth. Our help comes from Jesus, the greatest King *ever* who lives in Heaven!"

"I've heard of God and Heaven, but who is Jesus?" questioned Reggie.
"Jesus is God's Son who loves us and died on the cross to
show us that God always wants to forgive us of our sins.
He did that for you and for me and for everyone who believes in Him,"
explained the King.
"I don't even know Him. And He did that for me?"
Reggie put his hands on his heart.

ADMIT
↓
BELIEVE
↓
CONFESS

"How do we go to Heaven? Is it automatic?" asked the Princess.
"No, but it's as easy as learning your ABC's. You <u>A</u>dmit to God
that you have sinned, <u>B</u>elieve in Jesus's gift of forgiveness and
<u>C</u>onfess your faith in Jesus to other people."
"Oh, that's easy! Let's do it now," said Princess Pheona.

The King led the children in a prayer.
"Dear God, I sometimes do bad things and I need someone
to save me from my sins. I believe You sent Jesus to be
punished in my place. Thank you for doing this, Jesus.
I invite You to come into my heart and help me to live for You always."
After the prayer, the children became very happy!
In the morning they told the Queen and Mr. Peebles all about it.

23

"Good job, Princess Pheona!" Reggie high-fived her.
"Reggie, something good came out of my big problem with the pea.
It helped us to learn about sin and God's solution for it."
Princess Pheona was so happy that she jumped in the air!
"Oh wow. I feel so good on the inside. I have hope for the future,
Jesus to help me for the rest of my life *and* a comfy bed!"

Reggie and Princess Pheona danced and played
at the big celebration, but the real excitement
was the joy and peace that they now had in their hearts
because of inviting Jesus into their lives!

25

**Boys and girls, if you would like to say the same prayer that Princess Pheona and Reggie prayed to invite Jesus into your life, pray this prayer and mean it from your heart.**

## *"DEAR GOD,*

*I am a sinner and I need help from You
to save me from my sins. I believe that You sent Jesus
to be my Savior, and that He died
and was given the punishment that I deserved.
Jesus, please come into my heart and be my Lord.
Help me to live for You all the days of my life
and one day live with You in Heaven.
Thank you and I pray these things in Jesus's name.
Amen."*

- **If you prayed this prayer, write your name on the line below.**

- **Tell someone, a parent, a friend or a Pastor and experience the same joy that Princess Pheona and Reggie have!**

- **It's good to go to church and read the Bible to learn more about Jesus. He loves you very much!**

- **Follow him all the days of your life and talk to Him like a friend, even when you get older and He will be with you always!**

_____       _____
          My name                             Today's date

# A Note to Parents

This book shared the basics about sin and being born into the Kingdom of God.
To further explain God's Word, here are some scriptures that you
can discuss with your child.

• John 3:16 "Yes, God loved the world so much that he gave His only Son,
so that everyone who believes in Him would not be lost but have eternal life."

• Romans 10:9-11 "If you openly say, 'Jesus is Lord' and believe in your heart that God
raised Him from death, you will be saved.
10 Yes, we believe in Jesus deep in our hearts, and so we are made right with God.
And we openly say that we believe in Him, and so we are saved.
11 Yes, the scriptures say, 'Anyone who trusts in Him will never be disappointed.'"

• Romans 10:17 "So faith comes from hearing the Good News.
And people hear the Good News when someone tells them about Christ."

• I John 1:9 "But if we confess our sins, God will forgive us.
We can trust God to do this. He always does what is right.
He will make us clean from all the wrong things we have done."

• Mark 16:16 "Whoever believes and is baptized will be saved.
But those who do not believe will be judged guilty."

# Topics for Discussion with Children

• Share a time when you sinned (were selfish, hurt others or did wrong).
• Did you know what to do about it at the time?
• Do you know what to do about it now?
• How can you apply the story of The Very Sensitive Princess to your life?
• Discuss how Jesus died to show His love and how He offers the free gift
of forgiveness for our sins.
• How does the celebration of the children in the story relate
to the celebration that we experience when we are born again
into the Kingdom of God?
• Explain how we are born into this world, but can experience
a second birth and be born again.
• Discuss the importance of being baptized after being born again.

Made in the USA
Middletown, DE
07 July 2022

68759012R00015